DEFENDERS

PITCH INVASION

DEFENDERS
PITCH INVASION

TOM PALMER

With illustrations by
David Shephard

Conkers

First published in 2017 in Great Britain by
Barrington Stoke Ltd
18 Walker Street, Edinburgh, EH3 7LP

www.barringtonstoke.co.uk

Text © 2017 Tom Palmer
Illustrations © 2017 David Shephard

The moral right of Tom Palmer and David Shephard
to be identified as the author and illustrator of this work has
been asserted in accordance with the Copyright, Designs and
Patents Act, 1988

A CIP catalogue record for this book is available
from the British Library upon request

ISBN: 978-1-78112-731-5

Printed and bound by CPI Group (UK) Ltd, Croydon, CR0 4YY

*This book is dedicated to the memory of
Rose and Steve Wing.*

Seth stared in horror at what he saw on the spikes above the gate. Five human heads. Five heads dripping with bloody, severed flesh. Five faces with no eyes, only blank eye sockets where a crow pecked aggressively. It was a gruesome sight. And it stank.

1

Seth's phone buzzed as he was walking out of Maths. He knew it would be a text about one of three things.

(i) An alert from FC Halifax Town.

(ii) A message from his best friend, Nadiya.

or

(iii) A message from his mum.

The messages from his mum were the ones Seth had to focus on. She'd been ill and was now

at home recovering. Today was an important milestone – Seth's mum was waiting to receive her test results, to hear she was well again.

Seth found a quiet place at the foot of the school's main staircase to concentrate on what the message might say. He took a deep breath and checked his screen.

CLUB NEWS

Deadline Day. Halifax-born striker – Ian Oldfield, 20 – has left the Shay Stadium and signed for Liverpool for an undisclosed fee. The Egyptian forward, Yehir Jawaz, 32, will take Oldfield's place in the team. More info at fchalifaxtown.com.

Seth flung his phone into his bag and sprinted

up the staircase. All of a sudden, he was aware of the footsteps of two hundred Year 7s thundering towards him.

He was fuming.

He was livid.

He wanted to sprint the half-mile down the hill to the Shay Stadium and kick down the boardroom door. Selling Oldfield to Liverpool! What were they thinking of?

"Seth?"

Why would they sell him? Oldfield was their best player. He'd scored nine goals in six games this season. Halifax were top of the league.

"Seth? Wait."

Seth stormed on, picking up pace all the time.

"SETH!!!"

Seth stopped and turned round. Nadiya was there, breathless.

"Why didn't you stop?" she said, angry.

"They've sold Oldfield," Seth fumed. "That's why."

"Who?"

"Ian Oldfield. Our leading scorer."

Nadiya laughed. "So?"

Seth felt like his head was going to explode. Nadiya had no idea how important this was. He had to explain. He had to make her see why this was the worst thing that could possibly happen.

Still shaking with rage, Seth said, "So now Halifax have got no one to score goals for us ... except for some stupid Egyptian, or whatever he is, that we've signed from the middle east of nowhere and ..."

There was no laughter in Nadiya's eyes now.

"He might be good," she said coolly. "He might score more goals than Ian Oldfield ever did."

"No way." Seth shook his head. "Oldfield is a footballing genius. This Jawaz is just some bloke at the end of his career. Here for easy money. He'll be rubbish."

Seth's head had cleared a little. He'd blown off some of that white-hot anger.

But Nadiya looked less than impressed. She was scowling at him.

"What?" Seth asked, flinching.

"What you've just said is racist," Nadiya said.

Then she turned and walked off down the corridor, disappearing among the hordes of Year 7s.

2

Seth went after Nadiya. He'd have to move fast to catch her in the packed corridors of Year 7s swarming from one class to another.

"Nadiya!"

Wild thoughts swirled round his mind as he hurried.

What did Nadiya mean? How had he been racist? He wasn't racist.

Was he?

Seth knew he had no chance of getting past the dozens of students in his way, but he saw that Nadiya had stopped to allow Seth to catch her up. He went to her. Their friendship was too important not to.

Seth and Nadiya had more than an everyday friendship. In the last few months they'd investigated and solved two strange hauntings. In Halifax Seth had seen a massacre of Anglo-Saxon villagers. In London he'd seen the slaves who had built a Roman amphitheatre. These things had horrified him until he'd spoken to Nadiya about them and she had used her genius for history to help him.

Seth and Nadiya called themselves Defenders. And Seth didn't want to lose any of that.

"I'm sorry ..." he said. "Please. Just tell me. Why did you say that?"

"Forget it," Nadiya said. "This isn't a good day for you. We'll talk about it another time."

"No. I want to know," Seth insisted. "What did you mean?"

"Leave it. You're stressed, Seth. What with your mum's test results and stuff."

"So did you mean what you said?" Seth asked.

Nadiya nodded. "Yes I did," she said. "What you said was racist. *Some stupid Egyptian from the middle east of nowhere? Really?*"

The two friends stood and looked at each other for a moment, and Seth started to understand why his words had made Nadiya angry. He found he had nothing to say in reply.

"Have you heard from your mum?" Nadiya said, breaking the silence. "Does she know if the treatment worked?"

At the mention of his mum, Seth felt all the

energy drain from him. He shook his head. "No. But she's probably heard and is waiting at home to tell me."

Nadiya said nothing. The corridor was empty now, but for the two of them.

Mr O'Rourke, Seth's form teacher, peered out of the classroom, about to call them in. The annoyed look on his face faded when he saw Seth.

"Do you find out about your mum today?" he asked Seth. "I'm sorry. I overheard you two talking."

"Yes, sir."

Mr O'Rourke frowned as he put his hand on Seth's shoulder. "Why don't you sign out," he told him. "I'll sort it. Go home now. To your mum."

Seth just stood there. He wasn't sure what to do.

But Nadiya grabbed Seth, turned him round and pushed him gently in the back.

"Go," she said. "Home."

Seth walked along the deserted corridor, down the silent staircase, out of the school doors and home.

3

Seth put his hand on the tall wooden gate for a few seconds. He knew his mum would be sitting on the front step at the other end of the garden, waiting to speak to him. Maybe she'd have the piece of paper in her hands.

That's how Seth imagined it. His mum would be holding a letter from the doctors at the lab that told her whether she was well or sick.

He'd imagined this moment a thousand times

a day for the past month. Over and over, how both the different scenarios would play out. Seth wished he had someone else to help him. Another adult. His dad. But Seth had never known his dad.

His dad had died before Seth had even been born. All that Seth knew of him was the stories that his mum told him, the box of his dad's old superhero comics in his bedroom and the framed photo in the front room. It showed a man with a broad smile, rolled up white shirt sleeves and wild unruly hair, the exact same as Seth's.

As Seth hesitated, a shiny black nose appeared under the bottom of the gate, sniffing at the air.

"Hey, Rosa," Seth said.

His dog gave him a low friendly *woof* in response.

Seth pushed the gate open and bent down to greet her. But Rosa was a few paces back, her soft

toy womble at her feet. Seth knew she was daring him to snatch it.

Seth grabbed the womble, then held Rosa too, as she lunged at him for the toy. As he wrestled with his dog, he heard his mum laughing and looked up to the front door.

His mum was sat exactly where Seth had imagined she would be. But there was nothing in her hands – no letter or envelope. Seth could feel his heart hammering too hard and too fast in his chest. But he had heard her laugh. That had to be a good sign.

He stayed on his knees, with Rosa panting next to him.

"No news yet," his mum called down the garden. "We have to wait until Monday."

Seth felt that surge of heat and pressure in his head again.

"That's not fair," he shouted, as he stood up. "They said today. Thursday."

Seth couldn't bear the idea of waiting for four more days. He'd coped all month knowing that today was the day. He'd put all his energy into that. Now they had to wait again. And who knew if Monday would bring news or not?

Mum walked down the path to Seth. She pushed the gate shut, then hugged her son hard.

"Just four days," she said, her arms tight around him.

"But four days is for ever," Seth mumbled. "I can't wait any longer."

He felt his mum's grip loosen.

She sighed. "I can't either."

Seth and his mum fell silent. They both listened to a car drive past, a bird cheep in the cherry tree above them and another soft bark from

Rosa, who was leaning against Seth's left leg, her womble in her jaws.

"If it makes life easier, you don't have to go to school tomorrow," Mum said.

"School takes my mind off it," Seth admitted. "It's Saturday and Sunday I'm worried about. And ... and I thought we'd be celebrating at the weekend. I hoped ..."

A longer silence.

Breaking free from their hug, Mum stepped back and looked into Seth's eyes. There was a hint of a smile on her face.

"Do you remember when we were in the hospital in London and we made that list?" she asked.

Seth nodded. They'd made a list of things they were going to do when his mum had recovered. A list they'd compiled to help them look forward.

"What was first thing on the list?" Mum asked.

Seth smiled. "Cornwall," he said. "You said you wanted to go back to where you went on holiday as a kid. And when we got there, both of us could paddle in the sea."

Seth's mum's eyes lit up to match both their smiles.

"Let's go now," she said. "Let's go to Cornwall."

4

Friday morning. Seth stood with his mum and Rosa at Halifax station. He was excited about getting the train to Cornwall. Mostly.

The sun was just coming up over Beacon Hill. Seth eyed the top of the hill where he knew executed criminals were once left to rot as a warning to the rest of the town. He didn't look too closely. He didn't want to see decomposing corpses this week.

Seth checked his phone to stop himself looking. He'd had no messages from Nadiya. She wouldn't have left for school yet, so Seth he decided to message her. He grinned and took a selfie of him and Rosa, then sent it to her.

Seconds later, he got a thumbs-up emoji back.

Seth sighed. That felt a bit better. But, really, he wished he'd had the chance to talk to his friend face-to-face, so they could clear up their conversations the day before. He was still mortified at what she'd said.

And, deep down, Seth wished that he and Nadiya were in the middle of one of their investigations. That was when they got on best. Seth seeing ghosts. Nadiya telling him who the ghosts were, and where in history they were from. They were Defenders then, as well as friends.

"Kate!" A shout came from along the platform.

Seth watched as a woman with three children came towards them, smiling.

Rosa stood up, her tail wagging furiously.

Seth recognised them too. It was his mum's friend, Deborah and her kids. A teenager with long blonde hair. A girl with light brown hair, aged about six. And a boy, about three, who was holding a plastic light sabre and grinning at Rosa.

Seth noticed that Rosa was eyeing the light sabre. He pulled on her lead to let her know that he had his eye on her.

Seth's mum and her friend chatted for a couple of minutes while the kids made a fuss of Rosa.

"Philippa, come on, and you, Cooper," the children's mum said. "Niamh will be late for school." Then, as she gave Seth's mum a big hug, "I'll call you when you're in Cornwall, catch up properly."

The children stood up, patting Rosa and

tickling her ears. Then the Leeds train drew in on platform 2.

As the train pulled out of the station, Seth still refused to look up at Beacon Hill. He might be interested in his town's history, but he didn't want any of that undead stuff going on this week. But Seth had no idea that by the time the train reached Cornwall he'd be seeing things far more frightening than the corpses on Beacon Hill.

5

Seth and his mum changed at Leeds for the Truro train. It was a long journey to Cornwall. Seven hours.

Rosa slept at their feet, under the table, after an encounter with a man who'd got on at Sheffield. He'd sat over the aisle from them, and Rosa had taken against him, growling every time he shifted in his seat.

But he got off at Birmingham and now Rosa had relaxed and was snoring gently in her sleep.

"Tell me about Cornwall," Seth said.

His mum smiled. "We'd go to a seaside village called Portscatho every summer," she said. "It's got a little harbour and the houses are stacked up on the hillside behind it."

"Nice," Seth said. "What did you do there?"

His mum gazed out of the train window as they sped west. There were hills on either side of them, winding paths visible among the trees and the fields.

"We sunbathed," she said. "We walked along the coast. Fished. Paddled in the sea. I had friends in Portscatho too – other kids who stayed there. We'd swim together. Jump off the pier. And go to the hill fort."

Seth squinted out of the window, not fully concentrating on what his mum was saying. He'd

seen some figures walking along the paths. There were a lot of them, travelling west.

"It's a brilliant place, Seth," Mum went on, sighing a deep breath out. "Let's forget about Monday and the results. This trip to Cornwall will be nice. Agreed?"

"Agreed," Seth said. "Mum? Can you see those people walking in the hills?"

Mum peered out of the window. "Where?"

"On the sides of the hills," Seth said. "Look. There they are."

His mum gave him a quizzical look. "Seth," she said, lowering her voice. "I can't see anyone. Are they ... you know ... the ones only you can see?"

"Maybe," Seth replied, staring out at the figures.

His mum knew all about the things he could see. When it had started, she'd told him that his dad had had the same gift. It had helped Seth to learn that,

made him not be so afraid of what he could see.

Seth checked his phone – 12.30. Nadiya would be on lunch. She'd be free to message him.

"What do they look like?" Mum asked.

"Ragged. Dirty," Seth answered. "They're wearing rough clothes. Animal skins. They're too far away to see their faces."

"Have you seen ones like this before?"

"Maybe," Seth said. "They're wretched and exhausted, a bit like the ones in London, when you were in hospital."

"Before you were born," Mum said suddenly, remembering something, "I came this way with your dad. He saw things when we went to the Iron Age hill fort near Portscatho."

Seth swallowed. Any mention of his dad made his heart beat faster, especially when his mum compared Seth to him.

Seth's hands trembled as he messaged his friend.

"I need to ask Nadiya," he said. He wanted information and he knew that Nadiya was the person who would have the answers he wanted.

If people were walking west from Bristol to Cornwall. Dressed in ragged clothes. Animal skins. Who would they be? S

Nadiya's reply came back.

Refugees? Maybe Iron Age. Celts escaping Roman invasion. Or from Saxons. They went to settle in Devon and Cornwall. To get away from the invaders. Often lived in hill forts. Tell me more … N

Seth messaged back that he would if he saw more. He felt that buzz, that thrill of excitement that he had something to get his teeth into, something dangerous even. And, most importantly, it could be just the thing to take his mind off his mum's test results.

Seth understood that he was seeing a movement of ancient families fleeing persecution. Refugees. And they were moving south-west, in the same direction as he was.

Seth wondered what he would he discover when they reached Cornwall. He wanted to visit the hill fort his mum had mentioned, to go there because his dad had been there. And to see if there was a connection with the hill forts Nadiya had mentioned too.

6

The taxi from Truro station dropped Seth and his mum in Portscatho village square.

There was a cluster of neat houses painted white and yellow and blue. A village shop, a pizza café with tables and chairs outside, and a pub. Behind the village a steep slope led up to a church spire on the hill. Ahead of them, the sea stretched to the pale and distant horizon.

Seth's mum took a deep breath and grinned. "It

smells just like it did when I was a child," she said.
"Oh Seth, this is good. I feel better than I have for
ages."

Rosa was excited too. She was pulling at the
lead, letting out little whimpers.

"She wants the sea." Mum laughed.

Seth smiled, glad they'd come. Glad, too, to see
his mum so happy.

They walked down the slope, round the corner
of a tiny post office to a harbour wall, several
upturned boats in lines out of the water. Seth
dragged their holdall behind him. Its wheels seemed
to rumble like a freight train through the quiet
village. Mum took Rosa's lead and Rosa walked
gently alongside her, not pulling at all. Not like
when Seth held her. She was a good dog.

Seth scanned the seafront. Two boys were
perched on the harbour wall, dangling their legs

over the side. One of them had a football tucked
under his arm.

"It's beautiful, Mum," Seth said. "Like a
postcard."

Mum didn't reply.

Seth took that as a sign that she was tired. He
knew he had to make sure she took it easy.

"Come on," Seth said. "You're shattered. Let's
find our cottage."

"Yes," Mum said. "We'll have a proper look
around tomorrow."

They walked across the beach, a café with
tables on the cliff top above them. Seth let Rosa
off the lead. She sprinted at the sea and danced a
wild dog dance among the breaking waves, before
hurtling in crazy circles, leaving paw-print trails on
the sand.

After the beach, Seth led Mum and Rosa up a

track to some fields. The light was fading and the air was suddenly cooler.

"It's not changed much," Mum said again. "But that café is new. We'll have lunch there tomorrow."

Seth grunted. The holdall was heavier now he had to carry it. But he had insisted they take the shortcut to get his mum to their farm cottage quickly.

The farm was up a long track, trees either side closing over them like a green tunnel. Seth let his mum put her arm round him as they walked. She was so tired now he felt like he was carrying her. And the holdall.

A tall man appeared at the end of the track where the farm gate had come off its hinge.

"Mrs White," he said. "And Seth. Welcome! Let me take that bag. I'm Tim Marrak."

Tim took them to their cottage, which had

thick stone walls and wooden floors. Inside it was warm and felt cosy and clean. From its south side, Seth could see hills cascading down towards the vast sea.

He found the things his mum needed to get changed and into bed. PJs. Her toothbrush and toothpaste.

"Will you be able to get something to eat?" Mum asked.

Seth nodded. "There's that pizza place by the harbour. I'll go back there. Don't worry about me. You sleep."

"OK. Just don't stay out too late."

"Mum?"

"Yes, love?"

"The hill fort you mentioned on the train. Where is it?"

7

Seth ordered a Sicilian pizza from the café that overlooked the harbour. As he ate he stared out at the calm grey sea and wished – for once – he could have a settled mind. A head empty of worries. That would feel so good.

As Seth ate, Rosa eyed him and the pizza he was eating.

Seth shook his head. "Later," he told her.

The combination of pizza and sea views

was good, but not enough to distract him from his worries, so Seth paid the bill and moved on, following his mum's memories of how to reach the hill fort.

"Come on," Seth told Rosa. "Let's explore."

Seth wondered if he would see shadows at the hill fort. Shadows of Iron Age people. His mum had said his dad had seen shadows there. So why shouldn't he? And Nadiya had told him that the figures he'd seen from the train could be Iron Age people. Seth would go and see what this hill fort looked like, then he could report back to Nadiya.

Seth walked over some fields that backed onto the cliff edges, then inland along a tree-lined road with smart houses on either side. He was moving away from the beach and the sea. Then he saw a sign.

The Roundhill Ground
PORTSCATHO FOOTBALL CLUB
supported by the Football Foundation

"Mum didn't mention a football club," Seth told Rosa.

The sun had disappeared behind the hills to the west. Seth peered at the windows of the football clubhouse. There were no lights on. No cars in the car park.

The land at the far side of the football pitch was raised. Around it there was a huge line of tree trunks creating a fence. In front of that was a wide, deep ditch, a bit like a moat, but with no water in it. Seth thought it might be a giant adventure playground.

He let Rosa off her lead so that she could run across the pitch. She scampered and rolled, letting off steam after a day on the train and on her lead.

Seth wanted to get near to the strange wooden fence, work out what it was.

Closer now, he could see it behind the white football posts at the far end of the pitch.

There was a wide gap in the fence.

And, through that gap, Seth saw people. Coils of smoke rising from the tops of round huts with low thatched roofs. And then he understood what he was looking at. This was not an adventure playground made of great tree trunks. It was nothing of the sort. Seth realised that he was looking at a fort. A real Iron Age fort where people were living and working. It was the fort his dad had told his mum about.

Seth looked again and there – on spikes above the fort's gate – was the most terrifying sight he had ever seen.

8

Seth stared at the hill fort in awe.

At the small round hill that was really a fort protected by a solid ring of wooden stakes. At the gatehouse guarded by four men with heavy spears and swords.

But he stared in horror, too, at what he saw on the spikes above the gate.

Five human heads.

Five heads dripping with bloody, severed flesh.

Patches of skin rotting. Chunks of face falling away.

Five faces with no eyes, only blank eye sockets where a crow pecked aggressively at the last piece of eyeball.

It was a gruesome sight. And it stank. The smell reminded Seth of the corpse of a badger he had found in the woods with Rosa during the summer.

It was almost too much.

Seth's legs trembled as he kneeled down, his hands over his eyes.

But he wanted to overcome his disgust. He knew that these heads weren't real. That they, and the fort itself, were no more than shadows. That he didn't need to be afraid. He knew, too, that Nadiya would want to know about the hill fort. He wanted to speak to her, talk history with her, wanted to be working together.

And so Seth called his friend.

"Hi Seth," Nadiya said. "Are you in Cornwall?"

"Yes. Listen …"

"How's your mum?"

"Asleep. Listen …"

"Is she OK?"

"She's fine, Nadiya, but please listen to me. I'm at a hill fort. I can see its Iron Age shadows."

No reply. Seth knew his friend was listening now.

"I can see the hill fort, Nadiya," he repeated.

"Please," Nadiya said, urgent. "Describe it for me. Everything. What can you see?"

"There's a wooden fence," he told her. "It's made of tree trunks. They're on the top of a mound with a ditch round it."

Seth couldn't bring himself to mention the five eyeless heads.

"I'm going inside," he said. Then, "Nadiya. This is good. We could work out what it's all about, do what we did before. Defend the people who this thing – whatever it is – happened to."

"We could," Nadiya said. "Phone me when you can. Seth?"

"What?"

"Be careful."

9

Seth walked up to the hill fort gate, looked down at his feet as he passed the heads on spikes and then marched inside.

The hill top was about the same size as half a football pitch. There were seven round houses with foot-worn tracks between them. The houses were wooden and had low thatched roofs from which smoke was escaping. There were animals everywhere, loose and in pens. Goats. Chickens.

Dogs. Cats. Ducks. And Seth could see about a dozen people. Some of them were feeding the chickens, a child was chasing a duck and two men were beating metal by a fire.

Seth could see everything and everyone.

He described it all to Nadiya. "And I can see two small horses," he went on. "And there's a cart next to them. But it's a weird shape and looks like it won't carry anything but people."

"A chariot!" Nadiya gasped. "Is it a chariot?"

Seth walked on. He was glad that none of the shadows there could see him. Braver now, he went up to where the guards stood, still averting his eyes from the heads. He stood behind the shoulders of two of the guards and looked out.

He was shocked to see people outside the fort too. Sat near to where he had been standing on the football pitch.

"I can see people on the outside looking in," he told Nadiya, puzzled.

"Describe them."

"Well, the people inside look kind of tidy even though it's smoky and muddy here, with animals everywhere. But the people on the outside look really tired and dirty and hungry."

"Do you think they could be some of those who walked west?" Nadiya asked. "Like the ones you saw from the train."

"Refugees you mean?" Seth said. "From the Roman invasion?"

"Yeah."

Seth left the gatehouse area, Rosa close to heel. He went into the ditch and around the edge of the fort, talking to Nadiya all the time.

Then everything changed.

Rosa barked loud and sharp, just as Seth saw

two faces – boys – peering over the other side of the ditch, looking straight at him. The pair turned and ran away fast across the fields.

"Got to go, sorry," Seth apologised to Nadiya.

He had no idea if the two were boys from today – or shadows of the Iron Age. But he wanted to find out why they were running.

10

Daylight was fading fast as Seth watched Rosa climb the bank and disappear ahead of him in their pursuit of the boys. He scrambled after his dog, not sure what he would see or do when he caught up with her.

At the top, Seth found Rosa rolling on her back. One of the two boys was laughing as he scratched the dog's tummy. The other boy, a ball under his arm, was staring back at Seth. Seth recognised them. They were the boys from the harbour earlier that night.

"Hi," Seth said, watching Rosa.

Weird, he thought. His dog was behaving in the way she only did with him. She was completely relaxed, playful even. But she'd only just met this boy.

"I am Galip," the older boy said in reply. "This is my brother Aylan."

"And I'm Seth," Seth said, wondering where the boy's accent might be from.

"Do you live here in Portscatho?" Seth asked. "Or are you on holiday?"

Galip smiled and stepped forward. He put his hand out. It was a bit strange shaking hands with another boy. But it felt nice, too. Friendly.

"We have come here from Syria," Galip said. "We have settled in a house here." He pointed back to the village.

Then the two boys looked at Aylan, who was

now lying on the floor with Rosa, laughing as both of them rolled around on the grass.

"It is your dog?"

"Yes." Seth laughed, then, speaking to Aylan, he said, "I've never seen Rosa like someone as much as she likes you." Then he glanced at Galip's football, still under his arm. "Do you play football?"

Galip nodded. "We like Real." He opened the zip of his hoody to show the yellow and blue circle of a Real Madrid crest.

"I support Halifax Town," Seth told him.

Galip looked confused for a moment, then nodded. "They are a good team?"

Seth laughed. Then he said, "Sometimes. Yes."

Seth looked back at Rosa and Aylan again. They were still playing some daft game.

"Do you play football on the pitch there?" Seth asked. "By the hill?"

Galip shook his head, then stared at the hill fort. "No. Not there. On beach."

"Oh," Seth said. "OK." He really wanted to ask Galip why not.

"It is dark." Galip stared west at the horizon. "We must go home. Aylan. Come."

Galip put his hand out to Seth and they shook hands again.

"Come to the beach tomorrow," Galip suggested. "We play football?"

"Yes," Seth said. "I will."

Then the two boys were gone, swallowed up by the night. Seth glanced at the hill fort and knew he should be getting back to the farm. If his mum woke up she'd expect him to be there.

11

As Seth approached the farm he noticed a figure crouched down at the top of the track, partly hidden by the hedge that lined the road.

Seth slowed down, cautious. The five heads had scared the hell out of him back at the hill fort. Rosa sensed his hesitation, peered into the dark, then gave a short sharp bark.

"Seth?" a friendly voice called back. "Hello."

It was Tim. Now that Seth was closer he could

see that the farmer was fixing the gate, putting it back on its hinge.

"Nice evening," Tim said. "Been for a walk?"

Seth gazed at the small farmhouse with roses around the door. At the barns that had been converted into holiday cottages.

"I thought I'd visit the hill fort," he replied. "Give Rosa a run."

"She's a good dog," Tim said, ruffling Rosa's head.

Seth paused in case Tim said anything about the fort, but he didn't.

"I met a couple of boys," Seth volunteered. "Galip and Aylan."

Now it was Tim's turn to hesitate.

"Nice lads," Tim said at last. "From Syria."

"That's right," Seth said. "They had a football with them. We're going to have a kickabout tomorrow."

"Football?" the farmer said. "I'm surprised."

When Seth didn't reply, Tim said, "They have quite a story behind them, those lads."

"What do you mean?"

"They lived in Syria," Tim explained. "Both their parents were teachers. Then the war started and – this is terrible – their mother was killed in a bombing raid. Their house destroyed. Everything they owned, gone. Their dog too," Tim said with a glance at Rosa. "They were driven from their land by the government there."

Seth was speechless.

"So their dad took them away," Tim went on. "They crossed the land border to Turkey. Then over the sea in a boat. Imagine. I expect you've seen the news stories about families crossing the Mediterranean?"

Seth croaked, "Yes."

"Their boat capsized," Tim said. "The two boys were rescued by Greek fishermen. There was no sign of their –" Tim stopped, as if he couldn't bring himself to say the final horrible part of the boys' tragedy.

The night was quiet. Rosa lifted her nose to the sound of flapping wings as a pair of ducks circled the farm.

"They ended up in that camp in Calais," Tim went on. "Then a charity brought them over to the UK. They were lucky. Thousands of children don't make it ... you know that."

"Some of it," Seth admitted.

"They've come to live with a couple in Portscatho. But the whole village have taken them in, really. They're at school here. They've joined the Scouts. They're lovely lads. After all they've lost. But you say they like football?"

"Yes," Seth said.

"That's strange, because, up to now, they've refused to join the football club. I mean, they play at school. They're good, very good. But they won't go near the Roundhill Ground. My sister's the coach for the youth teams there and the brothers just aren't interested."

Seth frowned. *Why was that?* he wondered, remembering how the boys had been on the edge of the football ground, but not on it.

But Tim was packing his tools away, checking the hinge of the gate.

"I'm sorry," he said. "I've kept you. You'd better go and check on your mum."

12

Seth's mum was fast asleep when he got back to the cottage. He fed Rosa, locked the front door and closed the curtains. Then he slumped down in the front room on one of the little sofas. He liked the cottage. The inside walls were white-painted stone. The roof was held up by huge thick wooden beams.

Seth put his feet up on the table, connected to the WiFi and checked his phone.

Team news from Halifax Town for tomorrow's

away match. Seth scanned the starting line-up. The list of eleven names didn't look right without Ian Oldfield. Yahir Jawaz was in his place. But – after what he'd heard today about other people's lives – Seth didn't feel as sorry for himself as he had the day before.

Next a message from Nadiya. He must have missed it when he was coming back from the fort.

Any more news? N

Seth decided to phone her. But the reception in the cottage was bad. He needed higher ground. Rosa was snoring – loudly – and didn't even look up when Seth opened the door and slipped out. Away from the cottage, the darkness was extraordinary. The sky a mass of stars.

Seth used his phone torch to find the path up

the hill, where there was a bench at the top. He sat down and looked up at the blackness. The only sounds were the quietest of rustles. Seth was pretty sure that whatever animals were out in the dark were listening to him too.

"So what happened at the hill fort?" Nadiya asked.

"I met two boys," Seth said. "They were by the football club there."

"Are they on holiday too?"

"No. They live here." Then Seth told Nadiya what Tim had said.

Nadiya was quiet for a long time. "That's awful," she said. "Are you going to see them again?"

"We're playing football tomorrow. On the beach."

"Not at the football club?" Nadiya asked.

"I doubt it. They're not keen for some reason."

"Maybe you could help them?" Nadiya suggested.

Seth didn't reply. Something had just appeared above the hedge ahead of him. Something that filled Seth with such horror that he couldn't breathe, let alone speak.

"Seth? I said maybe you could help them ..."

Silence.

Seth stared blankly at the hedge-line between him and the road.

"Seth? I'm losing you," Nadiya said, irritation clear in her voice.

"I have to go," Seth choked.

Seth stared, hypnotised. The heads were here.

The horrible vision from the hill fort was now floating above the hedge. Their eye sockets were black. So black they were darker than the night sky around them. So dark they seemed to glow. And the

five heads were drifting towards Seth. All the time Seth was aware that this felt nothing like seeing dusty figures walking along a hillside or a mass of slaves in a Roman amphitheatre at a football stadium. These heads weren't the same as the shadows from the past he usually saw.

Seth could only find one word to explain how this gory vision made him feel.

Sick.

Seth felt like the onslaught of horror was crushing his brain inside his head.

He turned and ran. Not looking back, not breathing, just running. He needed to get to the cottage, shut the door and pray that, if he turned on every light in the place, he could forget the bloodied vision of the five unseeing heads.

13

It took a long time for Seth to fall asleep. Fear of the ghoulish vision he'd seen and worries about Galip and Aylan were playing on his mind. He wasn't sure if he'd dropped off or was still awake when it happened.

He'd heard shouting. Someone calling his name.

"Sethhhhhhh."

Confused and disorientated, Seth scrambled for

his bedside light. Expect he wasn't at home and so there wasn't one. And now he was in a messy tangle of sheets and blankets, as if someone had tied him up. Seth wrestled his way out of them as something above his bed caught his eye.

The five severed heads.

Seth twisted his own face away as drips of gore and flakes of skin fell on him, then retched as the stink of maggoty rotten flesh filled his nose.

"*Settttttttttth.*" A voice was calling.

Then Seth heard barking. Rosa. Where was she?

"Settttttttthhh." The voice called again.

A flash of bright light. And a familiar figure in the doorway.

"Seth? You're having a nightmare." His mum's voice. "It's OK. I'm here."

Seth sat up.

He could still see the image of the heads

hanging above him. They were burned into his eyes. He rubbed his face, stared at the light bulb to try to wipe out the horror.

His mum was next to him now. "Let's get up. Shake it off," she said. "Come on."

Seth did as he was told.

"We'll have some tea," Mum said. "It's nearly dawn. We can watch the sun come up."

They walked into the kitchen together and his mum put the kettle on, along with all the lights in the cottage. Seth thought how nice it felt. His mum was looking after him. He was the child again.

"Sit down," his mum said, and Seth sat. "What was your nightmare about?"

Seth shook his head. He didn't want to tell her. He didn't want to explain the voice, or the heads and the awful feeling of hopelessness that came with them.

"I can't," he said.

His mum smiled and patted his back. And Seth wondered if she thought the dream might have been about her. That he'd dreamed about her illness, playing out his fears about her dying. He was about to tell her that it was something else. But then, he thought, maybe all this was to do with his mum. About his worry over her test results. It could be. Dreams had a weird way of telling you the truth. Everyone knew that.

His mum put a cup of tea in front of him.

"Three sugars," she told him.

Seth tried to smile.

"Look," she said. "The sky's changing colour. Shall we turn these lights off and watch the sunrise?"

Seth was about to say no, leave the lights on. But, again, he didn't want to make his mum worry.

And he was starting to feel a bit stupid. What had happened had been a dream. Dreams weren't real. They weren't really the truth.

"Yeah. Go on," he said.

They sat and watched a slice of orange light form on the horizon, colouring the edges of the sea and the sky. Daytime was coming, bringing light to drive away the darkness.

But Seth knew that these golden stripes of light might not be enough to save him from whatever forces were coming his way.

14

That morning, Mum wanted to go with Tim on a tour of the farm as he fed all the animals. It wasn't something Seth would have chosen to do. He wasn't a kid any more.

"Please, Seth," Mum begged. "I want to feed the goats."

"Really?" Seth pulled an embarrassed face.

"Really. And the ducks. I like ducks."

His mum sounded like she was a kid now. A

little girl, not his mum. But Seth understood that if she could find anything to take her mind off her test results then she should do it.

"OK." Seth put on a broad smile. "Let's go."

They joined Tim in the barn with buckets of animal feed.

There were some other guests there – two younger children with their grandfather. Both hopping about with excitement.

The barn was full of sacks of feed, six canoes on a rack and – on the other side of a half-door – a horse gazing at them with solemn black eyes.

As his mum was feeding the goats, Tim came to stand next to Seth.

"I was talking to my sister first thing this morning," the farmer said.

"The football coach?"

"That's right. Helena. The under-13s have

training this afternoon at the Roundhill. Then a match tomorrow."

"Great," Seth said. "I'll go and watch."

"Well." Tim raised his eyebrows. "Helena was hoping you'd maybe ... play? She's missing a couple of players. If you fancied a spot on the bench, she'd be so pleased. What do you think?"

"It's shame Galip and Aylan won't play," Seth said. "It would be better if it was them, not me."

"It would. But maybe it'll encourage them if they see you taking part?"

Seth looked at his mum. She was kneeling down, her hands out flat as a goat hoovered up the feed. The two little kids were leaning into her, laughing. She had a big smile on her face too. Seth hadn't seen her look this relaxed – or well – in ages.

"OK," Seth said, turning back to Tim with a grin of his own.

15

Seth and his mum spent the morning walking around Portscatho, then going for lunch at the café that overlooked the beach.

Once they'd eaten, Mum said she was tired and wanted to go back to the cottage to sleep. So Seth took Rosa to the football ground. It was nice to have been asked to train with the local team. What was the worst thing that could happen?

As he arrived at the ground he glanced towards

the hill fort. Up to where he had seen the heads the night before. The sky was bright and clear. No ghoulish visions. Just an expanse of lush green grass, a white-painted club house and the hill fort as a backdrop.

But Seth did notice that the shadows of the people who had been outside the fort the night before were there, on the edge of the pitch. Not far from where Rosa was sitting chewing something.

Seth introduced himself to Helena, the football coach, and she invited him to join in.

The players started with a couple of warm-up laps of the pitch. Seth fixed his eyes on the grass as they ran. Then they did some short passing drills, moving closer and closer to each other, exchanging the ball faster and faster. Seth was pleased with himself. He felt like he was doing well, showing them he could play.

Eventually he miscontrolled a ball and had to run to fetch it where it came to a stop close to the ditch that surrounded the hill fort.

When he got there Seth saw Galip and Aylan. They were crouching in the same place they'd been hiding the night before.

Seth waved them over. But Galip shook his head and pointed to the side of the fort.

Seth followed the line of Galip's arm.

And they were there.

The five heads. Disgusting as ever. Seth could smell them too, that sickening maggoty-rat stench. Again, he could see the black hopelessness in their empty eye sockets.

Seth gave up trying to get the brothers to join in and tried instead to put the heads out of his mind. It was clear that no one else could see them. And that meant everything was OK. They were in

his mind and no one else's. Maybe they were to do with his fears about his mum, fears he couldn't talk about with anyone. Maybe they weren't even ghosts or shadows. Just because he'd dreamed about them didn't mean they were real.

Seth told himself that so long as no one else saw the heads he could live with them.

But when he went back to the football, Seth found that his game had evaporated. He misplaced passes. He failed to trap the ball. He spent more time apologising to the other players than doing anything constructive.

"It's fine, mate," one of them said. "We're just glad you're here."

Seth knew what that actually meant. They thought he was rubbish at football. They were just being kind. And that hurt, because Seth knew he could play way better than this.

It was the heads. That bleak feeling they gave him.

Seth stopped running after another ball he'd scuffed in the wrong direction. He stood still. He looked at the heads. He looked for Galip, but the brothers had gone.

Then Seth realised something, something that struck him hard.

Galip had pointed at the heads. He'd shown them to Seth. Now Seth understood quite clearly that the older brother could see them too. And if Galip could see them, then that meant Seth wasn't the only one seeing these shadows from the past. It meant they were real.

Seth shivered as the clear blue sky suddenly grew darker. A lot darker and a lot colder.

16

Seth made up his mind. He needed to go after the brothers. He had to know. Could Galip see the hill fort and its horror too? Was that why they never came as far as the football pitch?

"Sorry, I have to go," Seth shouted to Helena, then he plunged down one side of the ditch to be off through the fields. Rosa raced alongside him.

Seth ran as fast he could, but it was clear that

he'd never catch up with Galip and Aylan. The boys were long gone.

And so, Seth slowed from a sprint to a jog. He had a call to make. To Nadiya. He couldn't do this on his own. He'd talk as he went along.

Rosa stayed to heel, panting softly.

"Nadiya?"

"Seth? Are you OK?"

"I'm fine, but I need your help."

"Why are you so out of breath?"

"I'm running." Seth knew he was being short, but there was no time to waste. "Listen," he told Nadiya. "There was something about the fort that I didn't mention."

"Go on."

"When I saw it for the first time I saw some ..." Seth paused. "Decapitated heads."

"Heads?"

"Five of them. On wooden stakes. All bleeding and rotten. And I thought I was the only one who could see them, which meant it was just me, just me and a shadow, so it was OK. But now I think Galip, one of the Syrian brothers, can see them. And …"

"You want to know what they were for? The heads? I can tell you."

"Please."

"The villagers in the Iron Age fort put them there to scare strangers away," Nadiya explained. "The heads are a warning. They say, *We'll kill you. We'll cut your head off. We'll stick it on a spike. Don't mess*, basically. Those men could have been killed in battle. They might even have been sacrifices to the gods."

Seth stopped jogging. He could see across the bay to the village of Portscatho now. The sea was rougher today, water splashing up onto the top of

the harbour. He recognised two figures on the pier there. Galip and Aylan. They were on the harbour wall, indifferent to the waves, in the same place Seth had first seen them.

"Sacrifices? Like human sacrifices?" Seth asked. "Grim."

Nadiya didn't reply.

"So why can one of the brothers see them too?"

Another pause from Nadiya. Then she spoke. "When you saw the Iron Age people, you said some were outside the fort, looking in. Are they still outside?"

"They were," Seth said. He was walking out of the fields now. Past the café, into the outskirts of the village, five minutes from the harbour.

"So," Nadiya said. "I think the Iron Age people who lived in the hill fort didn't let the refugees in. That's why you can see that moment frozen in time."

"What do you mean?"

"It's a shadow," Nadiya said. "The shadow of a terrible event. The two brothers. They're refugees, aren't they? And so the refugees who weren't given a safe place to live – a refuge – in Iron Age times have come back. Along with those grisly heads. It's connected with Galip and Aylan. Or it could be."

"So what can I do?" Seth asked.

"You could do nothing," Nadiya suggested. "Just walk away and focus on your mum."

Seth thought about his friend's words. He wasn't far from Galip and Aylan now. He could see – quite clearly – that the older brother was comforting the younger one.

"But I feel like I want to help them," Seth said.

"Then you have to break the cycle," Nadiya said. "Like you did in Halifax. Like you did in London. You have to be a Defender again. You have

to confront the echoes of the past. The shadows.
Remember what you did before? You took them on.
You walked among them. And you quelled them."

17

Galip stood up as Seth approached. Aylan was squatting down with his arms around his knees.

"Hello," Seth said, holding out his hand for Galip to shake. "I have to ask you something, please."

"Ask," Galip responded, frowning.

Rosa walked over to Aylan and calmly pushed his arm with her nose. The younger boy looked up and patted her.

"Can you see the heads?" Seth asked, not knowing how to be anything other than direct.

Aylan began to sob, which made Rosa step back for a second and glance at Seth.

"I know what they are," Seth said.

Neither brother said anything.

Rosa nosed Aylan again, wagging her tail, as if she didn't want him to be sad.

Seth knew he had to explain. "So," he began, "about two thousand years ago in this village there was a hill fort. A kind of castle. And the people who lived there put heads, like the ones you can see, on spikes to frighten away people they didn't know – strangers."

"Why?" Galip asked.

"Because they didn't want new people ... to come from outside."

"Like us?" Aylan said in a flash, stroking Rosa

again and looking at her, not Seth. It was the first time Seth had heard him speak.

"They don't want us?" Aylan said, his voice flat.

Seth kneeled down. "No," he said. "That's not true. This village wants you. This country welcomes you. You belong here now." Seth hesitated. "But, in the past, people weren't always welcome. The ... the ghosts of those people are still here. That's why you can see the heads."

No one spoke for a while and the three boys stood on the harbour listening to the sound of the waves and two wooden fishing boats knocking into each other.

"I've seen this before," Seth said at last. "We need to walk into the fort, strong and together, and the shadows will go away. Then you'll feel safe again. Then you'll be able to play football."

"But what if the people in the fort hurt us?"

Aylan said. "What if they put our heads on spikes?"

"They won't," Seth said. "I promise."

Galip shook his head. "No."

Then Aylan stood up and spoke to his older brother in their own language. Seth wondered if they were arguing. At last Galip smiled and nodded at his brother. He turned to Seth. "Aylan asks if you will go into the fort first. He says that if you do and are not hurt, then we will go after."

"Into the hill fort?" Seth asked, trying to keep the wobble from his voice. "Alone?"

He'd tried to sound brave for the brothers, but now he felt terrified.

Could he do it?

He looked at the two boys. They were both staring at him, waiting for an answer. As they stood in silence, Seth remembered what Tim had told him about the boys' lives in Syria. Planes and helicopters

roaring overhead, dropping bombs on their city. Houses blown to bits around them. Their mother dead after a bombing raid. The loss of their father and having no idea if he was dead or alive.

Surely, Seth thought, he could face something that he knew wasn't actually real if these two boys had faced so much worse – the reality of war, of danger, of tragedy. Especially if his actions could help the brothers play the football they loved.

"I'll do it," Seth said and put his hand out for Galip. The boy took it, but pulled Seth into a hug, much more than a handshake.

Then, with Rosa back on the lead, the three of them agreed to meet at the Roundhill Ground the next day.

18

It was 5.30 a.m. Dawn.

But a thick sea-fret was stopping the sun from illuminating the land. The world was grey and cold and damp as Seth approached the hill fort.

He'd left Rosa at the cottage, ignoring her as she stared at him through the window pleading to come too.

Seth wanted to meet the brothers, then deal with the fort by himself. Galip and Aylan had

endured enough. Seth would do this for them. He
didn't want to be worrying about Rosa.

And so, once he had met them and told them
his plan, Seth left the brothers at the car park.
Aylan was shivering, disappointed not to have Rosa
to play with.

Seth walked quickly. His shoes were soaked
with dew from the long grass. But there was no
point in dawdling, or looking for excuses.

He had faced fear before. And it had felt a little
like this. But the horror of the five heads had got to
him. The fear they made him feel was stronger than
anything he'd known before. The only way to defeat
it was to remember what Galip and Aylan had been
through. They had suffered real fear and real horror.

But when he looked up at the fort and saw the
five bloody heads there again, Seth wondered if he
had taken on too much this time.

Could he overcome them? Could he be a Defender again?

The stench was appalling, a cloud of horror even thicker than the sea-fret. Seth could barely breathe.

He wanted to slow down. Stop. Turn around. Run away.

But he would not. He could not. Even though he had that feeling again, that exploding dense pain in his head and his gut, he knew he had to go on.

Seth thought he could hear a man's voice calling his name. But it wasn't a voice he recognised, so he blanked it and walked on, his legs like jelly.

Closer to the heads than he'd had been before.

Closer to the gatehouse at the hill fort.

He could see it all now. The wooden stakes. The guards peering down at him. The smoke rising from the thatched huts. The dull bang of metal being

hammered. The snuffle and bleat of pigs and goats. The bark of a dog.

And then – the heads. Now Seth confronted them at the gate. In their skulls those black shining holes where the eyes had been.

Seth hesitated.

The heads were lower now. So low he was face to face with death.

Should he walk on?

Or turn and run?

Had he done enough to quell them? That was the word Nadiya had used.

But there was that line in his head. *Face to face with death*.

Suddenly, Seth knew what that meant. Of course. He had been face to face with death for months. The prospect of his mum's death was the worst thing he'd ever had to tolerate. And he still

had to face it. He had to look death in the face for the next 24 hours at least. That was truly painful, so this was nothing. These gory heads were nothing at all. Not next to his fears about his real life. Not next to what Galip and Aylan had suffered.

Seth understood.

If he could carry on with the possibility of his mum dying and if Galip and Aylan could carry on their lives with the reality of their mum dying, then Seth could face this.

What could five rotten skulls do to him?

With his heart hammering, his throat constricting and his eyes blurring, Seth walked on.

19

Seth walked to the gate of the Iron Age fort, closer and closer to the five heads.

They stank. They dripped gore.

He stared at them hard, trying to take on their power, trying to show them he wasn't scared.

But he was.

He was terrified by the sight of them and the smell of them. They scared him more than they had near the farm and in his dream. He could see

maggots oozing out of the folds of flesh on their faces. They were so vivid that Seth felt like he had maggots on his own face. He scratched at his skin, felt vomit rise in his throat.

Then, in the distance, Seth heard the voice again. A man calling his name. But none of the heads' mouths moved as they loomed closer. The middle head was nose to nose with him now. The air was toxic and Seth thought he would faint. His eyes were watering. Or he was crying. He couldn't tell.

Seth stared hard at the pitiless black holes of the middle head's eye sockets. He could do this. He would be strong, he would win. He would do this for Galip and Aylan. Even for himself.

Then dark.

*

Seth dreamed he was in the sea. The water was black. Heavy waves were pushing his body, draining him of energy. He had to use all his strength to force himself up to breathe without taking in seawater. When he reached the surface of the water, he saw a little boat, Galip and Aylan clinging to its sides, crossing the treacherous dark sea at night. Their faces were pale, staring into the blackness.

Seth stared up at a sky that matched the darkness of the sea. There were no stars. No moon. And Seth wondered if he was dead already.

But then something came down from above the water. A man's hand with a white sleeve rolled up.

Seth took the hand and felt it pull him upwards.

Out of the water.

Out of the darkness.

20

When Seth came round, his clothes were soaking wet. He rolled over, thinking he was in bed, that the fort, the heads, the dark sea had been a dream.

"Seth."

It wasn't his mum's voice.

Seth opened his eyes.

Galip was kneeling over him. The sea-fret was swirling around behind him, brushstrokes of blue sky visible now. Then, a few metres away, Aylan was

staring in horror at the space above Seth and Galip.

Seth rolled over and looked above him. He knew now that he was not in bed, knew that he was on the grass of the hill fort, the five heads still there. He could see them, he could feel their presence.

"Seth," Galip said again. His voice was shaky. "Are you OK? You fell."

Seth nodded and stared at the heads. Then he stood up and threw a punch at one of them. His fist passed through it as if was nothing more than an image projected into the sky.

"We're safe," Seth said. "Look!"

Seth heard a laugh. It was Aylan. He had a half-smile on his face.

Galip helped Seth to his feet.

Seth looked at Aylan, then he lunged at one of the heads and pretended to slap its face.

Aylan laughed again, edging closer.

"Do you want to hit one of the heads?" Seth asked the younger boy. "They're not frightening now. Just shadows."

Aylan shook his head.

"You can," Seth said. "It didn't hurt me."

"It might hurt them," Aylan said. "I don't want to."

21

Four hours later, Seth sat on the edge of the football pitch watching the red and white stripes of Portscatho FC junior team against the lush green hill fort and the blue midday sky. He kept Rosa's lead short. She had her womble with her and was guarding it jealously from a nearby Labrador.

Seth's mum was next to him. She seemed full of a sudden energy. Smiling and chatty. Her friend, who'd they met at Halifax station, had called her

just before kick-off and their chat had given her a huge boost. Seth was impressed. There was still a day until Mum got her results, but she was behaving like she had everything to live for and didn't have a care in the world.

Seth wished he could feel the same.

"So, can you still see the Iron Age fort?" Mum asked.

Seth nodded. He described it to her – the ditch, the bank, the fence of wooden trunks. Then what he'd seen inside.

"But it's not – you know – troubling you?"

"No. Not now," Seth said, then admitted, "It was. There was something about it that was bad. But that's gone now. I can only see the fort."

And that was true – the heads had gone. Seth didn't tell his mum about them. Or his weird unconscious dream in the dark. All she needed to

know was that everything was OK now. That there was nothing for anyone to be frightened of.

"And is that why Galip and Aylan are playing today? Is that down to you?"

"A bit," Seth confessed. "But it's down to them really. They're brilliant players, aren't they?"

Mum nodded.

One thing that still worried Seth was that the Iron Age refugees had gone from the fort too, the group he'd seen on the first day. That puzzled him. Where had they gone?

A shout stopped Seth worries, brought his focus back to the action on pitch.

Galip had taken the ball onto his chest and had pushed his way past a defender. The score was nil–nil and time was running out. Everyone knew that this was a big moment in the match. For the team. And for Galip.

"Go on, Galip!" Seth stood up and yelled. "GO ON!"

Rosa dropped her womble and barked, then barked again – an echo of Seth's words.

Galip touched the ball with his right foot once, then struck it low and hard with his left. It whipped into the net.

Goal! A fantastic goal.

And the scorer was mobbed by his new team-mates.

*

After the game, Seth and his mum watched the families of the other players making a fuss of Galip and Aylan. There was a smiling older couple there too. Seth wondered if they were the boys' foster parents.

Everyone was slapping them on the back, singing songs and a few kids were doing daft celebratory dances. Someone went and got cans of pop for them all. And Seth saw Helena give both boys a booklet each, Portscatho FC handbooks. They were proper team members now.

Seth smiled. He knew, deep down, he'd done something good, he'd made a difference.

"Listen," Mum said. "While they're all busy, why don't we go and dip our feet in the sea?"

"OK," Seth said. He could tell by the tone of her voice that she had something to tell him.

When they were well away from the football pitch, he released Rosa from her lead, letting her sprint ahead of them onto the wide sands. His own legs heavy, Seth followed his mum down the path towards the beach.

22

Seth's mum led Seth down the hill and across the beach. The sea had turned and was coming in now, a surge of frothy water rippling up the sand. Just beyond that the water was being thrown up by the crazed shuttle runs of their dog.

They reached a cluster of rocks under the cliff edge.

Mum kicked her shoes off and flicked them up the beach. Seth did the same. They sat on one of

the smoother rocks. Rosa chased up the beach and retrieved them, placing them neatly at their feet.

All the way down to the beach, Seth had been worrying.

What was this about? Did his mum know what her test results were? Maybe she wanted to come to the sea to dip her feet because it was bad news. Maybe the ebb and flow of the sea would make it feel less bad. Or maybe she'd known the test results all along. But then, surely, she wouldn't have kept him hanging on.

Seth was confused. His body heavier still, like gravity had got stronger. He felt so tired.

"I didn't want to talk about my cancer up there," Mum started.

Seth noticed an edge in her voice. He didn't interrupt.

"Up there was about your new friends and this

village. But what I have to tell you now is about us, Seth."

His mum shuffled round to face him, next she put her hand on his shoulder. Then she was talking again.

"That phone call earlier wasn't my friend calling me for a chat. It was my doctor. She went into the hospital this morning to see if my results had come early and they had. And it's good news, Seth. No cancer. I'm all clear."

Seth stared at his mum's face. He could see sunlight reflecting off teardrops that were gathering in her eyes. They were sparkling.

Next, she put her arms out and Seth leaned into her. Gently, she hugged him. Just as the sea surged up the beach and covered their feet in cool Atlantic water.

23

Seth took Rosa up to the hill fort after his mum had gone to bed. They'd been out that evening for a pizza at the café on the beach and she was tired again.

But that was OK. Now, when his mum was tired, Seth knew she was tired and tired only. That was all. Nothing else. Nothing sinister. Not cancer.

Seth let Rosa off her lead so she could explore the hill fort. He watched his dog bounding about and

thought how he had never felt so happy. So relieved, so clear-headed.

When he reached the fort, he saw that the ghastly row of heads had gone, but everything else was still there.

Seth ghosted through the gate, past the guards and saw the people who lived in the hill fort with the refugees. They'd taken them in, were looking after them.

Seth smiled.

This shadow he was seeing was perfect.

Two thousand years ago, Portscatho had taken in refugees of the Iron Age. And now, in the 21st century, they were doing the same thing.

Galip and Aylan were in good hands.

Seth called Nadiya. His friend listened as he told her everything. The hill fort. The football. The brothers. His mum.

"You've missed one other piece of good news today," Nadiya said once Seth had finished.

"Have I?"

"I can't believe you've forgotten about the mighty Halifax Town!"

Seth gasped. He had. This was the first time he'd thought about them all day.

"Did we win?" he asked.

He heard Nadiya laugh. "You did," she said. "And guess who scored?"

Seth's first instinct was to say Ian Oldfield. But then he remembered. He'd gone to Liverpool.

"I dunno," he said.

"Jawaz," Nadiya told him with a laugh. "Your journeyman footballer."

"Jawaz?" Seth was taken aback.

"Yes. The match report says that he made a 'fantastic contribution to the team'."

Seth sighed. "I'm sorry," he said.

"Why?"

"You were right. I was being racist about him."

"Not really," Nadiya said. "You were angry about something else. Your mum was ill. It's OK."

Seth smiled. "Yeah, but I am sorry. I get it now."

"Get what?"

"Change. Even football teams change. New people come in and old people go and things can still be good. Things can be better. And it's the same everywhere. Even in this hill fort, this village."

"Agreed," Nadiya said.

Seth stared at the fort. He watched smoke rise from the thatched huts, saw the people gathered there. The ones who'd been there all along. The ones who'd been taken in.

Then, among them, Seth saw a man who wasn't

dressed like the others. He stood apart, but was still a shadow, a figure from the past. He was in dark trousers and a white shirt, sleeves rolled up.

Seth recognised him. His broad smile and wild hair.

The man waved, flashing that broad smile at Seth. The smile from the photo in the frame at home.

Seth waved back.

Then the man faded with the rest of the villagers.

Seth stared at the hill fort. It was just a round hill now, next to a village football club.

He put his arm round Rosa and smiled. Seth had done his dad proud. He'd shown the courage of a true Defender.

ARE YOU A HISTORY BUFF OR A HISTORY BUFFOON?

Take this hard-as-iron QUIZ to find out how much YOU know about Iron Age Britain!

1. Why did people of the Iron Age build hill forts?

A. Hill forts were high up and near to the skies where Iron Age people believed their gods and spirits lived.

B. Hill forts were their homes – they lived in them as places to protect them from their enemies.

C. Hill forts were pitches on which to play an ancient form of football, a game that lasted all week and had three teams of 19 players each.

2. Why did Iron Age people put decapitated heads on stakes at the gates to their hill forts?

A. They liked to keep the heads of dead friends and family near by to make sure they didn't forget them.

B. The heads were there as a "Welcome to Our Fort" sign for good spirits and friends.

C. The heads were there to drive people away. They were a warning sign that said "ENEMIES KEEP OUT!" or this is where your head will end up too.

3. Who or what brought an end to the Iron Age?

A. The Romans who invaded Britain, bringing elephants on their ships to intimidate the local people.

B. The Golden Age, famous for its golden head-dresses and golden sandals.

C. The Ice Age, when the world was covered in vast sheets of ice.

4. What made iron so important that it signalled a new age called the Iron Age?

A. It was used to make weapons and tools for farming.

B. It was used to build multi-storey homes and shops.

C. It was used to build boats so people could travel overseas and trade with other countries.

5. What shape were houses in the Iron Age?

A. Rectangular.

B. Triangular.

C. Circular.

6. Why did Iron Age people throw shields and weapons into rivers and lakes?

A. As offerings to the Goddess of Fresh Water.

B. They believed it was unlucky to use a dead man's weapons, and so they threw away weapons belonging to those killed in battle.

C. We don't know.

7. What the Romans feared most about Iron Age people were their chariots. Why?

A. Iron Age chariots were super-fast and could thrash anyone in any race!

B. The Romans thought chariots pulled by two horses were actually eight-legged monsters that would kill them.

C. Iron Age people were expert at using chariots in war.

8. Where did Iron Age people get their clothes?

A. From the Iron Age high street.

B. It was very hot in Iron Age times so they didn't wear any clothes.

C. They made them.

9. **What did people of the Iron Age use to write?**

A. Nothing. They couldn't read or write.

B. Quills, ink and parchment.

C. Chalk on slate.

10. **How did Iron Age people learn about their history?**

A. They used Romans as slaves who wrote their history books for them.

B. Talented poets memorised stories and told and retold them.

C. They didn't believe that any history before existed before them, so they didn't bother.

Answers on the next page ☞

ANSWERS

1: B

Iron Age people built forts to protect themselves against their enemies. Sometimes, everyone lived within the fort. Other times, the local population would retreat to the hill fort from houses outside the fort.

2: PROBABLY C

The Iron Age people didn't leave any written records of why they did this, but some Roman writings suggest it was done to scare their enemies.

3: A

The Romans invaded Britain in 43 AD. That invasion marked the official end of the Iron Age, although many people in Britain continued to live an Iron Age life for decades, if not centuries, after.

4: A

When people used iron to make their tools and weapons, it made them much stronger than the weaker metals and woods used before. Iron gave people the ability to make things, grow things and — when necessary — to fight with more power.

5: C

Iron Age houses were round. In fact, they are now called roundhouses. The Romans and Anglo-Saxons were more likely to build rectangular houses.

6: C

We don't know. A and B are ideas that could be true, but we can't be sure. What do you think?

7: C

One of the key tactics of Iron Age warfare was to drive chariots into the heat of battle to deliver the best warriors to fight where they were most needed.

8: C

Iron Age people made their own clothes from wool, leather and other natural materials.

9: A

The people of Iron Age Britain did not read or write. Most of what we know about them comes from the writings of Romans and other people.

10: B

Stories were passed from generation to generation by poets, known as bards. They entertained people by telling long, complex stories from memory.

BUFF OR BUFFOON?

If you scored 10/10

You're a top-class history buff. Seth and Nadiya will be glad to have you on their side as Defenders!

If you scored 5-9

You have more research to do before the Defenders will add you to their team!

If you scored 4 or under

Seth and Nadiya won't mind. They are history whizz-kids and will gladly give you a lesson!

Acknowledgements

This book – the third and final one in the *Defenders* trilogy – is dedicated to the memory of Rose and Steve Wing, the mum and dad of one of the friendliest families I have had the pleasure of knowing.

I also would like to thank my wife, my daughter, my agent and everyone at Barrington Stoke for all they have done to help make *Pitch Invasion* the story that it is.

Last, but not least, I'd like to thank the people of Iron Age Britain for building their amazing hill forts up and down the country. They are what inspired this story. I love visiting these forts and seeing the trenches and defences that Iron Age people dug to protect themselves. This website – www.arch.ox.ac.uk/hillforts-atlas.html – will help you to find out where your nearest Iron Age fort is. I hope you might enjoy imagining what Iron Age life of over two thousand years ago was like too!

About Tom Palmer

Tom Palmer is the author of over forty books for children. His books feature sport, spies, detectives, ghosts and history – and sometimes a combination of all these things!

In 2017 Tom embarked on a mission to visit lots of historical sites and tell the stories they inspired in his fiction. For *Pitch Invasion* Tom travelled to Castle an Dinas at Columb St Major, Cornwall, where there is an Iron Age fort that was built about 4,000 years ago. All the wooden posts that acted as fortifications have rotted away, but you can still see the three rings of ditches and raised ramparts. You also get a strong sense of how big the fort was – the centre of it is the size of a football pitch. Today, a local farmer uses this Iron Age fort to graze their sheep. What a brilliant way to keep the grass on an ancient monument short! It's an amazing place and Tom knew right away that it was a perfect setting for a Defenders adventure.

Tom lives in Halifax in Yorkshire with his family. He enjoys visiting schools up and down the country to talk about his books. Find out more at www.tompalmer.co.uk.

Have you read the rest of the

DEFENDERS

trilogy?

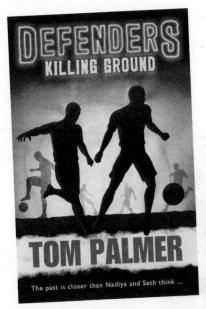

Out now!

Scorched circles, fire-blackened faces and fearful cries bring terror as a forgotten Viking massacre echoes down the ages.

Unless Seth and Nadiya can step up to the mark, their town may not survive.

Out now!

Seth and Nadiya's London holiday is fast becoming a nightmare.

The city is full of ghosts from Roman times – and Seth can see and hear them all …